W9-AMN-632

For James Alexander Egan
S. I.

For Marcus and Porridge
N. R.

First published in the United States 1996 by
Dial Books for Young Readers
A Division of Penguin Books USA Inc.
375 Hudson Street
New York, New York 10014

Published in the United Kingdom 1995 by Hutchinson Children's Books
Text copyright © 1995 by Shirley Isherwood
Pictures copyright © 1995 by Neil Reed
All rights reserved
Printed in Hong Kong
First Edition
1 3 5 7 9 10 8 6 4 2

Library of Congress Cataloging in Publication Data
Isherwood, Shirley.
Something for James / by Shirley Isherwood ; pictures by Neil Reed.—1st ed.
p.   cm.
Summary: When James receives a mysterious package
containing something that is rustling about, his toy animals help
him coax it out.
ISBN 0-8037-1914-0 (trade)
[1. Animals—Fiction. 2. Toys—Fiction.]
I. Reed, Neil, ill. II. Title.
PZ7.I775So   1996   [E]—dc20   95-37383   CIP   AC

The illustrations for this book were prepared with watercolors.

Something for
JAMES

Shirley Isherwood

PICTURES BY *Neil Reed*

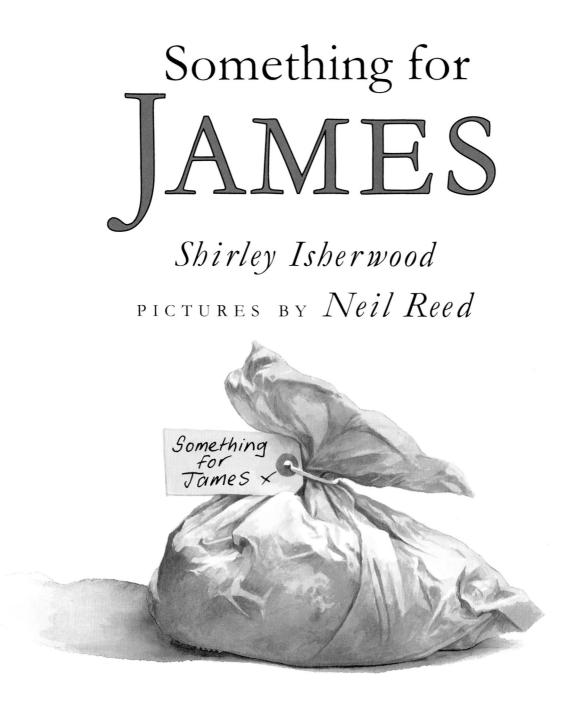

Something for James x

DIAL BOOKS FOR YOUNG READERS

New York

One day something arrived in a brown paper bag for James. Elephant found it on the doorstep. It was a large brown paper bag, and the top was twisted tightly around so that Elephant couldn't see what was inside. But she heard a rustling sound, and then a hiccup.

Elephant put on her glasses to read the label that was tied to the bag. "Something for James," she read.

James had gone for a walk with Winston. They went walking together every day.

Elephant sat on the doorstep, and waited as patiently as she could. Something in the bag sighed.

"Oh, my," said Elephant, and very carefully she opened the bag and peeped inside.

Two big dark eyes gazed back at her for a moment, and she caught a glimpse of two long soft ears.

"Are you a rabbit, dear?" asked Elephant. The soft fluffy ears certainly *looked* like rabbit ears.

Whoever was in the bag didn't answer.

"Perhaps you're a puppy, dear," said Elephant, for she could see a nice round tummy. But whoever was in the bag wasn't a puppy. Winston was a puppy, and he barked and scampered about. Whoever was in the bag sat quietly and didn't stir.

Elephant closed the bag, and put it carefully back on the doorstep. Then she set off down the street to find James and Winston. "Something in a bag for James," she said as she went, so that she would remember everything. "Long soft ears, big dark eyes, nice round tummy. Hiccuping and sighing."

Then, when she had almost reached the street corner, she suddenly thought, Suppose the something in the bag is a fierce something. Sometimes, fierce things lie quietly and then *pounce!*

She hurried on as quickly as she could, and was very glad when she heard James and Winston cry, "Turn left!" and saw them come marching into sight.

Elephant ran to meet them.

"Hurry home right away!" she said. "There's something sighing in a brown paper bag. It might be a terrible fierce pouncer!"

"A what?" said James.

Elephant tried to gather her thoughts, but before she could tell James about the big dark eyes, the nice round tummy, and the hiccups, Winston had set off down the street, barking loudly.

"I'll get that terrible fierce pouncer!" he said as he ran. James and Elephant ran after him, but by the time they reached the house, Winston had picked up the bag and was racing around and around the yard. Elephant and James caught up with him by the fishpond.

Winston was very pleased with himself, and dropped the bag at James's feet. At once the bag rolled down the sloping lawn and into the reeds that grew by the edge of the water.

"Oh, my!" said Elephant.

The bottom of the bag was very wet. As Elephant lifted it out with her long trunk, the paper tore and the tip of a soft gray paw with pink velvety pads peeped out.

"It isn't a terrible fierce pouncer," said James as he and Winston followed Elephant to the house.

Winston said nothing, but he thought, Well, it *might* have been.

Elephant put the bag on the rug to dry. Something in the bag sighed and then sneezed.

James opened the bag and peeped inside. "Please come out," he said, but something just covered its eyes with its ears and curled into a ball.

Elephant put the tip of her trunk into the bag, but something just rustled about in a worried manner. "He really should come out," said Elephant. "His paws are very damp."

James went upstairs to look for Bear, and found him asleep on the windowsill.

"Bear," said James, "something has arrived in a bag, and he won't come out."

Bear woke up at once. "How exciting!" he said as he jumped from the windowsill.

"How mysterious," he said as he padded down the stairs.

"How extraordinary," said Bear as he looked at the bag that lay rustling on the rug.

"We thought that it might have been a terrible fierce pouncer," said Winston.

"Terrible fierce pouncers don't arrive in brown paper bags," said Bear. He was very old, and knew almost everything.

He put his paw into the bag, and the worried rustling suddenly stopped. Bear's paw had the comforting smell of muffins and cocoa.

Two long ears appeared from the bag, and two big eyes, followed by the round tummy and soft gray paws with velvety pink pads.

James, Winston, Elephant, and Bear were very glad to see him.

"But what is he?" James whispered to Bear.

"He's a Something," said Bear. "It says so on the label. 'Something for James.'"

Elephant brought Something a mug of warm milk. Something drank it in one gulp, and then went back into his bag.

"Better leave him to settle in his own time," said Bear, and went back to his windowsill.

James, Elephant, and Winston went to bed. Winston slept at James's feet, and Elephant slept by his pillow, as they had always done. Everyone slept soundly, but woke up some time later at the sound of rustling. Opening the bedroom door, they saw Something making his way upstairs, dragging his paper bag behind him.

Everyone went quickly back to bed so that he wouldn't be alarmed by the sight of the faces looking at him through the banister.

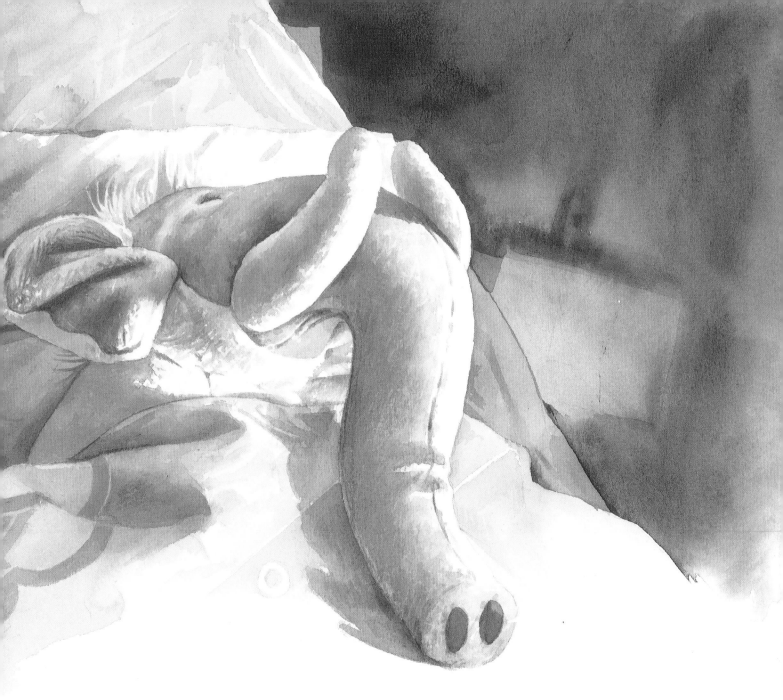

Soon after, James felt Something creep quietly onto the pillow.
"Good night, Something," said James. Something gave a
happy sigh as he snuggled down under the blanket.
One of his soft gray paws was still a little damp.